Dorothy AND TOTO

The Disappearing Picnic

by Debbi Michiko Florence

illustrated by Monika Roe

PICTURE WINDOW BOOKS
a capstone imprint

Wizard of Oz: Dorothy and Toto
is published by Picture Window Books,
a Capstone Imprint
1710 Roe Crest Drive
North Mankato, Minnesota 56003
www.mycapstone.com

CAPS34784

Library of Congress Cataloging-in-Publication Data
Names: Florence, Debbi Michiko, author.
Title: Dorothy and Toto. The disappearing picnic /
by Debbi Michiko Florence.
Other titles: Disappearing picnic
Description: North Mankato, Minnesota : Picture Window Books,
a Capstone imprint, [2016] | Series: Warner Brothers. Dorothy
and Toto | Summary: Dorothy and her dog, Toto, go on a picnic
but are puzzled when their food goes missing.
Identifiers: LCCN 2016011087| ISBN 9781479587049
(library binding) | ISBN 9781479587087 (paperback) | ISBN
9781479587124 (ebook (pdf))
Subjects: LCSH: Gale, Dorothy (Fictitious character)—Juvenile
fiction. | Toto (Fictitious character)—Juvenile fiction. |
Picnics—Juvenile fiction. | Weasels—Juvenile fiction. | CYAC:
Picnics—Fiction. | Weasels—Fiction.
Classification: LCC PZ7.1.F593 Do 2016 | DDC [E]—dc23
LC record available at http://lccn.loc.gov/2016011087

Designer: Alison Thiele
Editor: Jill Kalz

illustrated by Monika Roe

Printed in China.
007729

Table of Contents

Chapter 1

The Best Basket

Dorothy Gale and her dog, Toto, live in the Land of Oz. Magical things happen in Oz.

Every morning Dorothy waters her garden. She talks to her flowers.

"I think today is a nice day for a picnic," Dorothy said one warm, sunny morning.

"What is a picnic?" Rose asked.

"It is a meal you eat outdoors," Dorothy said.

"What will you eat?" Daisy asked.

"I don't know," Dorothy said. "Toto and I need to go to the Picnic Shop. The shopkeeper sells picnic baskets filled with food."

"Where will you have your picnic?" Fern asked.

"We will look for a spot in the woods," Dorothy said. "We will look for the perfect, sunny spot."

Toto jumped up and down.

Dorothy finished watering her garden. Then she and Toto walked to the Picnic Shop.

"Hello, Dorothy and Toto," the shopkeeper said. "How may I help you this morning?"

"We need a picnic basket, please," Dorothy said.

The shopkeeper showed Dorothy
and Toto all kinds of baskets. Some
were big. Some were small. One basket
had wheels!

"There are so many baskets,"
Dorothy said. "How will we choose?"

Dorothy picked up a big green basket. She wobbled. "Oh, dear!" she said. "I think we need a smaller basket. This basket is too heavy."

Next she picked up a pretty yellow basket. Toto yipped.

"This basket is much easier to carry,"
Dorothy said. "But it doesn't look like
it holds much food. I hope we will
have enough!"

Chapter 2

The Perfect Spot

Dorothy and Toto skipped into the woods. They soon saw their Munchkin friend Milton.

"Hello, Milton," Dorothy said.

"Hello, Dorothy and Toto," Milton said. "Where are you going?"

"We are going on a picnic. Would you like to join us?" Dorothy asked.

"Our basket is small and doesn't hold much food. But we will share what we have with you."

"Thank you," Milton said. "You are very kind. But the ducklings and I are going swimming today."

"That sounds wonderful," Dorothy said. "Have fun!"

Toto barked. The ducklings quacked.

Dorothy and Toto walked farther into the woods. They looked for the perfect picnic spot.

The first spot was shady and cold. The next spot crawled with ants.

Finally Dorothy and Toto came to a clearing in the woods. It was grassy, soft, and warm.

"This is the perfect picnic spot," Dorothy said.

She opened the small basket and pulled out a big blanket.

"Oh, my!" Dorothy said. "How did that big blanket fit in there? We must have a MAGIC picnic basket."

Dorothy spread out the blanket. Toto barked. Food! He wanted food! The long walk had made him hungry.

Dorothy laughed. "Be patient, Toto."

Next Dorothy pulled out a plate of
fried chicken. She put it on the blanket.
"Look at this chicken, Toto!" she said.
"This is going to be a tasty picnic."

Dorothy smiled and turned back to the basket to get more food. When she turned, a nearby bush shook. Out dashed a weasel! It snatched the chicken and ran back into the bush.

Dorothy didn't see it. Toto was too surprised to do anything.

Dorothy turned around with a bowl of apples. She saw the empty plate.

"Oh! Toto!" she said. "Did you eat the chicken?"

Toto shook his head.

"I know you are hungry," Dorothy said. "But please wait until I get all of our food on the blanket. Then we will eat together."

Dorothy put the apples on the blanket. She turned back to the basket to get more food.

The bush shook again.

Chapter 3

Toto's Troubles

Quick as a flash, the weasel popped out. It snatched the apples and ran back into the bush.

Dorothy turned around with a plate of sandwiches. She saw the empty bowl.

"Toto," Dorothy said. "You ate the apples too?"

Toto barked loudly and growled. He pointed at the bush with his nose.

"That wasn't very nice," Dorothy said. "We're supposed to share the food. Please wait."

Dorothy put the plate of sandwiches on the blanket. She turned back to the picnic basket. This time Toto was ready . . . or he THOUGHT he was.

Toto stared at the bush. He pawed
at the ground. But the weasel snuck up
behind him — ZIP! — and stole all of
the sandwiches.

"Toto!" Dorothy shouted.

Toto spun around. Dorothy frowned at the empty sandwich plate.

Dorothy put cheese and crackers on the blanket. They disappeared.

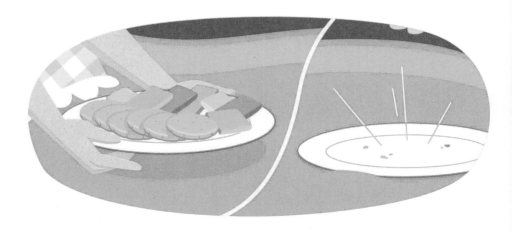

She put three pudding cups on the
blanket. They disappeared.

The cake and chocolate cookies
disappeared too.

Again and again the weasel ran past Toto and stole the food. Again and again Toto tried to catch the weasel. Dorothy never saw the little bandit.

"It is a good thing this is a magic basket," Dorothy said. "It holds a lot of food. But I would like to eat too, Toto. I'm hungry!"

Toto was hungry too. He was sad that Dorothy thought he had eaten all of the food. How could he tell her he didn't do it?

Chapter 4

Food to Share

"How can you eat so much, Toto?" Dorothy asked. "You must have a big tummy ache by now."

Dorothy reached into the basket again. She put a watermelon on the blanket and turned back to the basket.

SQUEAK! SQUEAK!

Dorothy spun around. She raised her hands. "Ah ha!" she cried.

There was the weasel, trapped beneath the heavy watermelon.

"So it was YOU!" Dorothy said.

The weasel wiggled itself free, then ran back into the bush.

Dorothy hugged Toto. "I'm sorry I thought you ate the food," she said. "Let's try this one more time."

Dorothy put the basket in the middle of the blanket. She took out hot dogs, potato chips, and bananas. She took out salad, beans, and cherry pie.

Toto watched.

Finally the basket was empty.

"Little weasel," Dorothy called. "Please come out."

The bush shook, and a little brown nose poked out. Out came the weasel — slowly. It bowed its head low. Then it held out a flower for Dorothy.

"I know you're sorry," Dorothy said. "If you want some food, just ask nicely. We have plenty."

The weasel nodded and squeaked, and another weasel crept out of the bush. And another . . . and another . . . and another!

Toto barked and wagged his tail. Dorothy laughed.

"Mrs. Weasel!" she said. "No wonder you needed so much food."

Dorothy, Toto, and the weasels shared the delicious picnic. They enjoyed the good food. They enjoyed the warm sun. They were thankful for new friends in the Land of Oz.

About The Wizard of Oz

The Wizard of Oz follows young Dorothy Gale and her little dog, Toto, who are magically taken by tornado from Kansas to the Land of Oz. Dorothy sets off on the Yellow Brick Road and meets Scarecrow, Tin Man, and the Cowardly Lion. They join her on a dangerous journey to meet the Wizard of Oz, whose powers may help Dorothy return home.

The Wizard of Oz is one of the most beloved stories of all time. The book was written by L. Frank Baum and published in 1900. It was made into a movie starring Judy Garland in 1939.

Glossary

bandit (BAND-it) — a robber

duckling (DUCK-ling) — a young duck

patient (PAY-shehnt) — calm during difficult times

perfect (PER-fekt) — without a problem or mistake

picnic (PIK-nik) — a meal that is eaten outside

snatch (SNATCH) — to grab quickly

weasel (WEE-zel) — a long, thin furry animal with short legs

Use Your Brain

1. In what ways was Dorothy's little yellow picnic basket magic?

2. Describe the perfect spot that Dorothy and Toto found for their picnic.

3. Dorothy is a very kind person. Give examples of things she says or does that show her kindness.

About the Author

Debbi Michiko Florence writes books for kids and teens in The Word Nest, her writing studio that overlooks a pond. Her work includes two nonfiction books for kids and a chapter book series, Jasmine Toguchi. Debbi is a California native who currently lives in Connecticut with her husband, her little dog, and two ducks. She loves to travel around the world with her husband and daughter. Before she became an author, Debbi volunteered as a raptor rehabilitator and worked as an educator at a zoo.

About the Illustrator

Monika Roe was born with a passion for art. She grew up in a small town on California's central coast and couldn't wait to get to the big city, where she earned a degree in graphic design and entered the world of advertising. She worked as an award-winning art director and creative director in Los Angeles, California, and Indianapolis, Indiana, before becoming a full-time illustrator. Monika's studio is located in the redwood forest of California's Santa Cruz Mountains. There she creates illustrations for people throughout the world while her pug snores loudly in the background.

CHECK OUT MORE

Dorothy AND TOTO

ADVENTURES!

What's YOUR Name?

The Hunt for the Perfect Present

The Disappearing Picnic

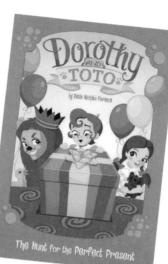

Little Dog Lost

For MORE GREAT BOOKS go to
www.mycapstone.com